A Wizard in Love

By Mireille Levert

Illustrated by Marie Lafrance

TUNDRA BOOKS

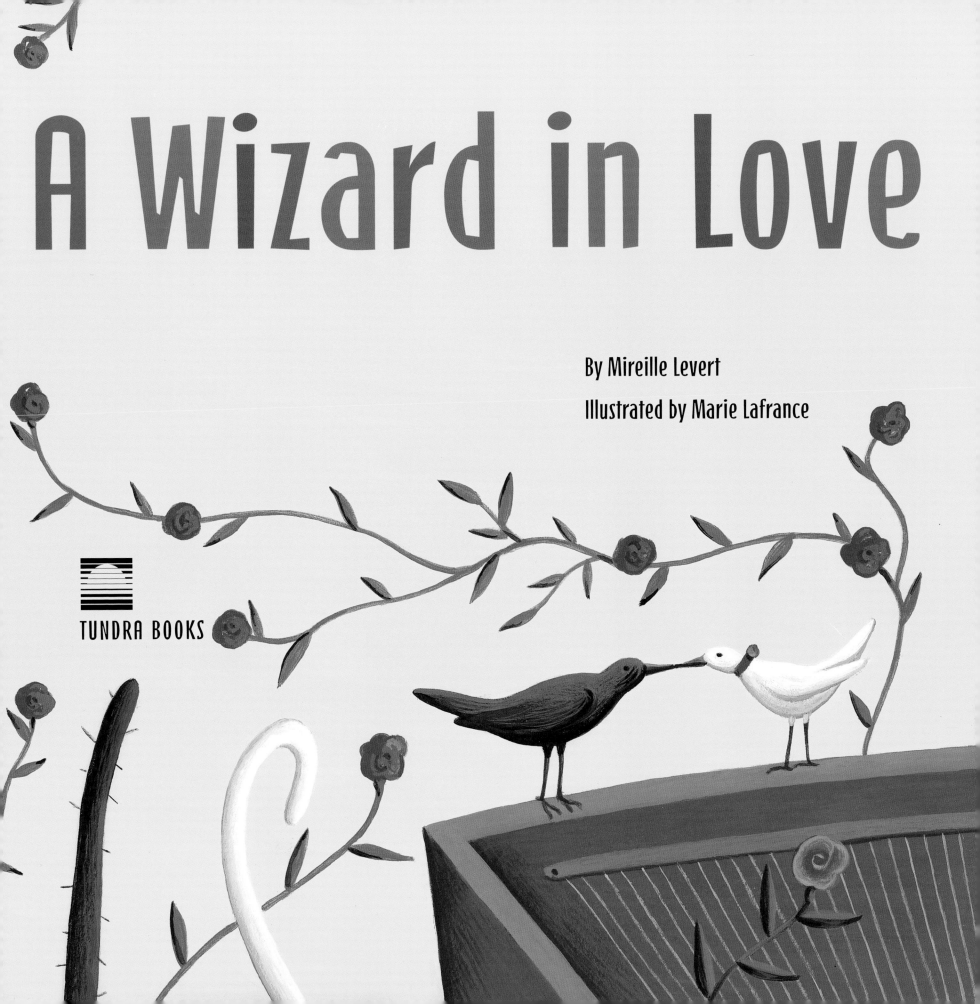

Published in Canada by Tundra Books,
75 Sherbourne Street, Toronto, Ontario M5A 2P9

Published in the United States by Tundra Books of Northern New York, P.O. Box 1030, Plattsburgh, New York 12901

Library of Congress Control Number: 2008903001

Library and Archives Canada Cataloguing in Publication

Levert, Mireille
[Sorcier amoureux. English]
    A wizard in love / Mireille Levert ; illustrations by Marie Lafrance.

Translation of: Le sorcier amoureux.
ISBN 978-0-88776-901-6

    I. Lafrance, Marie II. Title.

PS8573.E956355S6714 2009   jC843'.54   C2008-902074-X

We acknowledge the financial support of the Government of Canada through the Book Publishing Industry Development Program and that of the Government of Ontario through the Ontario Media Development Corporation's Ontario Book Initiative. We further acknowledge the support of the Canada Council for the Arts and the Ontario Arts Council for our publishing program.

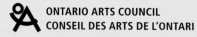
ONTARIO ARTS COUNCIL
CONSEIL DES ARTS DE L'ONTARI

Printed in Singapore

1 2 3 4 5 6   14 13 12 11 10 09

A Wizard in Love

To Marie and her own rogue paintbrush! – Mireille

*For my father, a retired wizard, and for my mother,
who plays the piano – Marie*

Hector was a retired wizard. He lived happily in a dilapidated house at the edge of the forest with his cat, Poison. Hector had at least three naps daily, and he growled contentedly after each one. He couldn't remember the last time he'd had his wizard friends over to visit, or even the last time he'd cleaned his house. The shutters were always firmly shut against the sun, and the telephone was always unplugged. Hector and Poison were content to spend their days watching TV and munching cookies.

One morning, as Hector slept amongst the cookie
crumbs, he was startled by a horrible noise.
He opened one eye, then the other. The sound
was so dreadful, Hector couldn't fall back to sleep.
He tried covering his ears. He stuck his head in
a flowerpot. Nothing helped. Hector could still
hear the ghastly noise. It made him furious.

He threw open the shutters. Rays of sunshine
hit the wizard square in the eyes (which only put
him in a worse mood). At first, Hector couldn't
see anything, but as his eyes adjusted, the outline
of the old abandoned house across the road
appeared. As if by magic, the house was all
spruced up. Someone had moved in. And that
horrible, dreadful noise hammering at his brain
was coming directly from the house.

Hector marched across the road. The freshly painted house glimmered
in the daylight, but as Hector approached, all he could think about
was the horrendous racket. He peeked through the open window.

In the middle of the living room was a beautiful woman with a lovely smile, singing as she played the piano. "How hateful!" Hector growled. "This must be stopped."

The wizard raced home and ran up the stairs to his attic.
He opened the cupboard where he kept his magic books,
potions, and powders. He found the big book of spells
and flipped through its pages: how to make hair fall out,
how to make someone grow warts, how to make teeth ache,
how to make itching powder, *how to bake an evil cake!*
"This will stop the infernal racket!" said Hector.

Hector put aside his magic wand and set about mixing ingredients. Soon, the large cauldron in the hearth began to bubble and the potion overflowed, covering the kitchen in foam. Nasty blue smoke rose up and seeped out of the chimney. "Yum," said Hector.

A tad of green powder here, a touch of red powder there. Hector poured the potion into a bowl, mixed it until it settled, then placed it in the oven. While it baked, the cake thundered and rumbled and gave off a foul odor.

Poison, always curious, sneaked a taste. Suddenly he began to grow. His front paws sprouted into leathery dragon wings. He opened his mouth to *meow*, but instead he breathed fire.

"Smarty pants," grumbled Hector. He grabbed his wand and waved it over the baffled cat. Poison was restored to his furry self.

By the afternoon, the cake was finished.
Hector was ready to put his evil plan into action.
"I'm rather proud of my plan," he said to
Poison, as he arranged the cake on a platter.
"This will get rid of all that annoying beauty."

He plucked a handful of flesh-eating flowers,
and, balancing his hideous cake, he set out for
the pretty house across the road.

Hector grabbed the doorknocker and knocked.
It chimed a pretty musical tune. Hector muttered
a curse. The door opened, and there she stood;
the beautiful woman with the splendid smile.
Hector gritted his teeth, he turned his head,
and he presented her with his gift.

"Hector, your neighbor," he said. "I made you
a fine cake to welcome you to the neighborhood."

"How kind of you! I am Isobel. Please come in." Hector was taken aback by the lovely Isobel's voice. It was clear as water in a babbling brook and gay as the song of a bird. He faltered. He no longer felt quite so angry. She smelled wonderful, like lilacs and cinnamon. He let the flowers fall to the ground and slowly stepped inside.

"Come," said Isobel, taking him by the hand. The house had such an air of happiness that Hector quivered. She set Hector's cake down on a small table and led him to the piano.

They sat side by side on the piano bench. The charming Isobel guided Hector's fingers over the piano keys. Suddenly, he remembered a time before the closed shutters and the unplugged phone and the filthy house. He played one note and then another. Isobel gazed deep into his eyes, and, sweetly, softly, she began to sing.

As she sang, the music began to work its spell on Hector. He forgot his evil cake and wicked plan, and he began to smile. He couldn't remember the last time he felt this way, but he recognized the feeling. He was in love!

Hector and Isobel sang into the wee hours of the night. Their songs delighted their neighbors, Poison, and everyone who heard them. And for all we know, they are singing still.

The End